A French Cowboy
First Encounters
A Short Western novel
By Eric Lafayette
Edited by
Vicky Vaughn Zeitlin

In your hands you have a short, small, compact and very exciting book to read, a book that will bring you great moments of pleasure. It is an Eric Lafayette trademark to go directly to the essentials or to the action. Whether it is a short novel, an analysis of great events or a poem you will always have in your hand a dense, intense nugget with a touch of philosophy and wisdom in the background,

Furthermore we know that you will want to share your pleasant experience with friends or family members and give them the gift of intellectual pleasure and wisdom. For that purpose we have a special program: It is a very simple program that will enable you to buy two copies of one of Eric Lafayette's book for a discounted price allowing you, to give the second book to one of your friends.

Acknowledgements:
My warmest thoughts to Vicki Vaughn Zeitlin and Jan Gabrielson for their kind and helpful support

Tribute

    "A French Cowboy" is a tribute to Clint Eastwood and Louis L'Amour as well as a wink to my younger years.

I am from France, and when I was young, European people---most notably French people---idolized Clint Eastwood especially for his first Western movie "A Fistful of Dollars," which was made before Americans recognized him as a star.

A few years later in a bookstore in Paris I was surprised to find a few Louis L'Amour western novels in French. I read all of the titles available in France, fewer than ten at the time, and enjoyed them very much. Then, while visiting the USA for the first time, I flew to many cities, and in each airport bookstore I found Louis L'Amour titles in English. I read them eagerly.

Although I was French, in my younger years I lived the life of a cowboy in the allegorical sense of the term, and now I am writing books like Louis L'Amour did. The story you are about to read is purely fictional, but the philosophy behind the story is for the most part based on concepts I cherish
Eric Lafayette

This book is using larger fonts to make reading pleasant for readers from 7 years old to 107 years old

The short novel
A FRENCH COWBOY
-FIRST ENCOUNTERS-
was published by Eric Lafayette
using the Createspace.com process
ISBN:9780615913131

TABLE OF CONTENTS

Chapter 1: First Encounter

Riding just ahead of his pack horse with his dog trotting at his side, Alan cleared the ridge of the last hill. He saw a burned-out wagon in the valley below. He studied the scene, then got closer and circled around, studying tracks and signs that might reveal what had happened. The wagon was still standing half burned, close to a small wooded area and a creek. He dismounted and searched the wagon. The only thing that might show who these people were was a leather purse pinned under a board. The purse contained two sheets of paper.

There were no clothes, blankets, or tools, but half a dozen books were strewn on the ground around the wagon. Books were precious to him. He collected them and put them in a bag on the pack horse. Checking the surroundings, he saw no sign of danger, but noticed two small wooden crosses near the remains of the burned wagon. Each was on top of a mound of freshly turned earth that appeared to be a grave. He said a short prayer for the two unfortunate travelers. As he scanned the scene, he was able to guess the main elements of this tragedy. A large party of Indians riding unshod horses had overwhelmed the pioneers. Judging from blood on the grass, the pioneers had put up a good fight and probably killed or wounded a few Indians. But the fight was too uneven. Westward-bound wagons must have stopped at the site and their passengers buried the dead people. From the way the graves were dug and from the amount of moisture still in the dirt he concluded that they were dug very recently, perhaps the day before. He found no large campfire and believed that the wagons' owners left in haste, for fear of another Indian attack.

It was still early afternoon, so he decided to stay and see if he could gather more information about these people. He set up his camp in the woods where his horses could be picketed and hidden. He then fed Blinky, his dog.

Secure at his camp site, he was deep in his own thoughts when Blinky came to him growling in a strange way. Blinky continued to growl, whimper, and point his nose toward a large tree. Alan followed his dog deeper into the woods to a fox den hidden by bushes, where his dog became even more agitated. Generally it took more than a fox den to make his dog that restless.

Alan unfastened the thong of his gun and began to talk to his dog to quiet him down when he heard what he thought was a human voice sobbing softly. Alan pushed the bush away and saw a few blond hairs, the collar of a green shirt, and what appeared to be a very young boy, who continued to cry.

Puzzled he called softly, "I am a friend. We are safe now. The Indians are gone. You can come out." The little boy did not move. Alan repeated, "I am a friend. We are safe now. The Indians are gone, and you can come out." The little boy still did not move or acknowledge Alan's presence. He appeared to be in shock. Alan said to his dog. "Blinky, I can see you feel that our little friend is hurt. I know that you want to help him. I want to help him too, so here is what we are going to do."

He spoke to his dog while giving him hand signals. "Go down there and stay next to him."

Blinky crawled into the den and gently licked the boy's face and hand.

Alan waited and his heart skipped a beat when he saw a little hand barely moving but patting the Dog's head. He knew that the love of an animal was a hundred times more powerful that ten hours of conversation, and he said so to his dog.

He scanned his surroundings again and after a few minutes called his dog back. He told the boy, "This dog, whose name is Blinky, is your friend now and he is going to come out, and you will follow him because he wants you with him and you want to be with him."

Alan called Blinky back and the dog crawled backward. The boy tried to pull himself out but could not, so Alan squatted on his heels and eased him out of the fox den. As soon as the boy was out he hugged Alan and sobbed uncontrollably.

Alan took him into his arms and held him against his chest.

Five minutes before, Alan was a lonely, cool, fiercely independent cowboy and now he was overwhelmed by emotion. He wanted to comfort and protect this little boy more than anything he had wanted for a long time.

As he carried the boy to his camp, he was happy that the boy's parents were already buried. He made some hot herb tea and prepared some food while continuously talking to the boy, telling him the name of his horses and asking Blinky to stay close to the boy.

Once the boy was fed and almost clean, Alan decided the sooner the boy could put the tragedy behind them the better. He took the boy to the graves and explained to him that his parents had gone to heaven and that they were watching over him from high above with all their love. Alan told him that he has been sent by God to be his protector and that he would care for him. He decided that although it was quite late, it would be a good idea to move his camp and to put some distance between the scene of the tragedy and the boy. It would also keep the boy busy, which might soften the boy's anguish.

Alan believed that now was time to enter into a conversation with the boy. So far,

Alan had done all the talking. "Hi, would you like to give me a hand packing my blankets and things. As you can see, I have two horses and I could use a little help."

"Yes," the boy said.

"By the way, my name is Alan. What's yours?"

The boy said, "Billy Musgrave."

"Okay Billy, can you ride a horse?"

"I don't know. I have never ridden before. We only had two oxen to pull the wagon."

"Would you like to try?"

"I . . I don't know."

Alan said, "I'll tell you what, I will help you get on the horse, I will walk and I will lead the horse and never let him go. You'll be safe and it will be your first riding lesson. Let's finish packing and go."

As soon as they had packed, he put the boy on the packhorse and led both horses. Alan began to walk toward a little hill about one mile away. While walking, he gave Billy Musgrave his first riding lesson.

Chapter 2: The First Riding Lesson

"Now Billy, you are on a horse and you can see that I am walking next to you. You're on the packhorse, sitting on a blanket with the packs around you. You will see that it is a very pleasant and comfortable way to get around. How are you feeling, Billy?"

"I'm OK."

"Sit straight with your shoulders back, let your legs dangle and relax. We are at a walk. It's a slow and comfortable pace. I put a bridle on the horse so that you can pick up the reins, one in each hand. Keep your hands apart and low. Because this horse is very well trained it is very easy to let him know what you want him to do."

"If you want to go left, move your left hand a little bit to the left away from his neck to bring his nose to the left as you look to the left. Now both your head and the horse's head are pointing to the left. Same thing if you want to go to the right. Good Billy! You can see you are going to the left now, how do you like it?"

"I like it."

"I have to warn you that my packhorse Jimmy is trained to stay with the other horse and you will have difficulties moving him away from the other horse, so don't try it. When you're a bit more advanced, I'll teach you to ride with both reins in one hand.

"Another thing you need to know that is essential in riding is that you direct the horse when the horse is in motion, which means when he goes forward. If the horse is stopped and you turn his head to the left, he will not turn left, he will only turn his head to the left.

"You direct a horse the same way you change the flow of a creek. You cannot direct a pond to flow left or right, but you can direct a stream to go left or right by changing the direction of its banks. That's because there is a flow, which means energy. It's the same with a horse. You need to have the energy and willingness to go forward. Then and only then you change the direction and make the horse go where you want to go. Do you understand so far Billy?"

"Yes, I think so."

"Do you want to try to do a little bit of trot? I'll jog along with you."

"Yes, I can try."

"Put your shoulders back a little bit more, don't lean forward at all, and let's trot."

Alan clucked the horse into a slow trot and he saw that Billy was doing well. He told him, "You're doing fine Billy. If you feel you are sliding a little bit to the left or the right, grab the strap in front of you that is holding the packs on the shoulders of the horse and pull yourself back to where you want to be. You will notice if you lean forward you are going to bounce too much, so stay with your shoulders back. How do you like it Billy?"

"I like it."

"Billy, I am going to get on my horse, and we will continue riding a little bit."

Alan got on his horse, followed the creek, and aimed the little troop at a clump of trees at the top of a small hill. He began a very slow trot and of course Jimmy the packhorse followed.

He said to Billy; "Billy you are a born rider, you are doing very well. You will become a very good rider." For the first time he could see a smile on the boy's face. The boy seemed proud and happy to be a rider. Then they walked and trotted again, and Billy was totally focused on riding, which was helping him for now to forget the scary times he had endured not so long ago.

It was a joy to see this little blond man trying to stay on this horse while bouncing around a little bit, but riding successfully with the cooperation of the gentle packhorse.

When they arrived at the little wood, Alan dismounted and helped Billy dismount from his horse. He explained to him that they were going to be very busy setting up camp. "First Billy, come close and watch as I take care of my horse, and then I will help you with your horse."

Billy followed Alan like a shadow. He helped put the saddle and the packs next to a tree.

"I will show you how to hobble the horses so they do not run away, and I will introduce them to you."

The hobbled horses started to graze. "If there is one thing I would like you to remember forever, it is that there is only one way to handle horses or ride them and that is gently. In the future you might see people who are rough with horses in order to train them.

Sometimes they get quick results, but they will never have good horses that will give their heart and soul to their owners. Because horses don't speak and don't understand your language, they don't do what you ask. It is your task to make yourself understood by your horse."

"In general, horses have no desire to disobey after they are trained. A horse wants to obey you and to please you. It is only when they don't understand you that they can't do what you are asking them to do. Most riders get upset because they think it's the horse's fault. You must remember that it is never the horse's fault. It is always the rider's fault because he was not able to communicate with the horse in a way the horse could understand.

"Your first and absolute duty when a horse does not want to do what you are asking is to observe the horse and try to understand what he is trying to tell you by not following your orders. Let me introduce you to our friends.

The horse you rode, you know his name; it's Jimmy. He is twelve years old. He was given to me because he was biting the owner and the owner was beating him. The owner was saddling him and tightening the girth in a brutal manner which caused the horse pain. But it was really easy to make him stop biting and make him into a good friend. He hasn't even attempted to bite for the last two years; he found his natural calling which is to be gentle and friendly.

The other horse is my horse Flame. I bought him from a lady friend who has some of the best horses in America. I have had him for five years now, and I have taught him all the tricks I could.

"I found Blinky on the outskirts of a town, and he started to follow me. I asked the fellows in town and they told me that his owner had left him behind when he left town. Well, since then he hasn't ever left my side, and he will be your best friend too.

"Let's feed the dog first because after he has eaten he'll sleep for a while and then stand guard while I sleep. We'll eat and then I'll stand guard. Around eleven at night he'll wake up and start his watch, so you see there will always be somebody to watch over you."

Alan built a fire as he talked to the boy, and as the fire crackled he felt the gentle heat, a symbol of human life in the middle of a beautiful and wild environment. These were enchanting moments for him and they always brought happiness to his heart.

Alan continued to talk to the boy, "Tomorrow, we'll head to a town because I want to buy a saddle for you so that you can continue improving your riding. The town is about one day's ride from here and that will give you more experience riding."

While Alan prepared dinner he kept talking to the boy, explaining to him who he was.

Chapter 3: Alan Growing up

"Billy, my name is long: Yves Louis Marcel Maurice Alain de La Roche. I am the son of a French count and that makes me a viscount. Upon arriving in America in 1866 when I was 16 years old I took the name of Alan Laroche because my French name was too complicated and did not make sense in America. I was raised in the southwest of France in the Bordeaux region, a part of France not only well known for its wines but also for its scholars and cultured people. This region gave France one of its greatest thinkers: Montaigne.

"My father Jacques was one of the most erudite men in France and wanted to pass his own thirst for knowledge to us his children. I had a very good tutor, but my father, who had a talent for sharing his knowledge with his children, involved himself in teaching us in a manner that engaged our interest completely. With him we studied Greek and Latin. These seemingly arid fields of knowledge were made easy and fascinating by studying the lives of the great heroes of the ancient world such as Ulysses and Julius Caesar. Mathematics and physics were simple and always taught with practical examples. I remember one that gave us great pleasure because it was manufacturing small catapults. A catapult is a device that can throw stones great distances.

"Of course, the boys trained in all sorts of arms. Not only were the rifle and the pistol important, but also the sword, the bow, and the crossbow, as well as boxing the French way. My father was a very kind man and he often told me that I had great skill with rifles and pistols. Both girls and boys were taught to ride and shoot. All of Jacques' children had full schedules that kept them busy all day learning and staying physically active. Even though their activities were pleasant, their purpose was to teach them in ways that would prove useful throughout their lives.

"We had a wonderful life and we knew it. After we had supper with our parents, we made a little circle and sat around our wonderful mother Eleanor. We were like a little group of rivals trying to impress our very learned mother with the lessons we were taught during the day.

"We were all mesmerized by our mother. Not only was she beautiful, she was a talented reader. She could read in a way that brought to life the heroes she was describing.

"My father was more a moralist and a scientist and used to tell us, 'My dear children, remember that curiosity for new things and new thoughts is the mark of intelligent people, so be curious and avid learners all your life.'

"Now that I am an adult and have studied the lives of many famous people, I am impressed to realize that in all the steps of our education our parents were deeply involved, which was rare in most families. Not only my father but also my mother introduced us to the lives of great men and women such as Joan of Arc and Julius Caesar to instill academic knowledge as well as moral rectitude. In our family reading was a daily pleasure.

"Although my father stayed most of the time at his property near Bordeaux, he went to Paris a few times a year. Once a year in the summer he took his entire family to the capital where we spent a couple of months going to grand balls and beautiful receptions. We the children were not invited to these events. But thanks to our father and nanny, we were often able to peek at the grand balls and magnificent hunts, hiding behind our devoted Nanny who kept us hidden behind doors and drapes.

"Each time he went to Paris, however, the economic and political situation seemed to worsen. His friend Victor Hugo was fighting tooth and nail against tyrants and was thinking of going into exile. Most learned people were appalled by the constant oppression of intellectuals. During this time period France switched back and forth between Republic and dictatorial, short-lived monarchies. The 1850s and 1860s in France were a very trying time. Because of all these troubles, my father's financial situation was not very good.

Chapter 4: Alan's Journey to the USA

"My father Jacques had heard wonders about America from his friend the Marquis de Lafayette, also known as 'the hero of the two worlds.' He was keen to send me to America, which was the first true beacon of liberalism and democracy on earth at this time. After the Civil War in the USA was over, my father, after consulting with my mother and me, decided to send me to America. I was sixteen years old then and delighted to be on my way to the USA, which we called America. I was very excited. My tutor and I took a boat from Bordeaux to London and then to New York. My father told me that he had given me money that was hidden in a money belt my tutor was wearing. The day before my departure my father told me that he had taught me all he could and that with all my skills there would always be a way for me to be successful in life.

"The journey on the ship to the USA did not go well. We encountered a huge storm and all the passengers were sick including me. One morning I discovered that my frail old tutor was dead. I took the money belt, went to the ship's Captain and told him that my tutor was dead. After a short prayer the body was thrown into the sea as the Captain had very little time to spend on anything but repairs to his boat and completing the voyage to America. There was an important silver lining in my two months' journey. During our long trip I was able to learn English from a young Englishmen who had boarded the boat in London.

"At last the ship reached New York and I disembarked with a couple of trunks at my side and did not know what to do. Fate was about to make a decision for me.

"A smiling young man named Harry offered to take me to a nearby Inn. I accepted. The trunks were loaded onto a hand carriage and I started towards town with my new acquaintance.

"Suddenly six rough looking people armed with clubs appeared out of nowhere and attacked me and I was ready to fight them, but Harry seized me from behind and restrained my arms while the others knocked me unconscious with their clubs. I eventually woke up with a terrible throbbing in my head and rose slowly. I checked for my money belt and realized that it was gone. I was in a land I did not know anything about and had no money at all. My trunks were gone along with all my possessions. I had just learned a precious lesson: never trust anybody--- especially strangers with friendly smiles.

"As I recovered, I touched my face and found it was covered in blood. A passerby, an older man took pity on me and asked what had happened. When I described my ordeal the old man explained that passengers along the docks were frequently picked up by thugs and robbed. The older man could see that I was already recovering well from the ordeal and asked what I would do now and I said I had no idea.

"The kindly stranger said, 'What are you good at?'

"I said, 'I was told that I am very good with pistols and rifles.'

"The stranger said, 'Let me write a note for you to take to a friend of mine.'

"He wrote a note, read it aloud, and gave it to me. The note said 'Please John, do me a small favor and give this young man a bed for a night or two. Perhaps you could use him to clean guns and help you in your gunsmith shop.' The note was signed George Elan. George looked at me and said: 'Follow this street for six blocks and you will see a store with guns in the window. Enter and give my note to Mr. John Smith, a short, slim fellow in his sixties.'

"I followed the street and entered the store where I was cordially welcomed by Mr. Smith, who gave me a bed below the counters in the shop. John Smith then helped me clean my cuts and gave me bread, milk and molasses for dinner. In the following days, the shop owner told me he was very impressed by the care I gave the guns and by my respectful attitude with the customers who were trying out the guns in the shooting gallery behind the store.

"I answered, 'My Father felt very strongly that we always had to do a perfect task at anything we were engaged in, one of the very rare things that enraged him was to see that we had not done a thorough job at any task he gave us.' Mr. Smith went into the shooting gallery and put a large nail on one of the targets with its head protruding.

"He asked me to shoot the nail so that it would be driven into the cork board. I was a bit anxious and although I aimed carefully I missed the nail, which was about 100 feet away. I tried again and missed. The shop owner took the hand gun and in less than one second and with one bullet drove the nail into the board. We walked to the target and the owner showed me that my bullets were very, very close to the nail and for a first attempt that was an extremely good result.

"You see Billy that was my first stroke of luck in America, two decent human beings helped me. One helped me because my father had given me an important skill the gift of being a good marksman. The other helped me because he was a kind man that saw a kid that has been beaten and robbed. If you are very good at something in this vast and beautiful land called America, people will respect you and will need you. Of course that is not the end of the story of my life and since you are such a good listener and when we have time I will tell you many more stories about this shooting gallery and how I worked in a circus, learning tight rope walking, knife throwing and many other skills."

"I will tell you the rest of the story another day you as are falling asleep, which is a good thing. Go to sleep and Blinky and I will watch over your sleep"

The next day, after Alan made stirrups with straps, they   both went trotting and cantering under Alan's careful eye and wise teaching toward the next town.

Chapter 5: Going to Town

They arrived at a pleasant small town and took their horses to a stable where Alan told Billy, "Always care for your horses first. Let's give them some grain." Alan unsaddled the horses and brushed them while at the same time giving advice to Billy. Then they walked to the biggest store in town, which was called the East and West Emporium, and browsed through their large inventory. Alan bought a used saddle for Billy and renewed contacts with some of his friends.

Near the stable, there was a corral where cowboys were breaking wild horses. They went to watch. It was an amazing sight with bucking broncos and cowboys flying in the air. While Billy watched in awe, Alan went to the Sheriff, an old acquaintance of his, explained the story of Billy and gave him the papers he found in the wagon mentioning Billy's parents. The Sheriff told him, "Alan, the kid could not be in better company than yours. Keep him with you, stay in touch with me and I will try to track down his relatives."

When Alan returned, Billy was very excited. He told Alan, "There is a horse that nobody can ride. Every cowboy has been thrown to the ground. He is so beautiful. I know you can ride him; you are the best rider in the world." Alan said, "Look Billy I have old bones and I am not as flexible as I used to be so I don't think I can do it.

"Billy interrupted with a yelp and said, "Look he has thrown another rider to the ground. You are the only one who could do it."

Alan said, "Well, we need a third horse for you. You could be right."

John, the owner of the horse was an old acquaintance. Alan observed the horse carefully for a few minutes then said to John, "If I tame this horse would you give it to me for free? That would be a very good deal for you because by the end of the day he will have sent all your cowboys to the doctor with broken bones."

John answered, "Alan you are my age, and I am not crazy enough to try to ride him but if you want to try and if you tame him he is yours."

Alan had learned all about horse behavior in France and in the circus. He quietly told Billy that he had noticed that the horse was afraid of the strange shadow that was created when a rider was on his back. This new shadow had the shape of some monster lurching on his back ready to attack him.

"I read about this problem in the ancient Greek and Latin books my father gave me to read. In ancient times there was an extraordinary conqueror whose name was Alexander the Great. When Alexander was young he tamed a horse named Bucephalus who was one of the wildest of all. Alexander noticed that it was the combined shadow of the rider on his back in addition to its own shadow that looked like a beast of prey that panicked the horse. I am guessing that this horse has the same problem."

Alan led the saddled horse to the edge of the corral, made him face the sun and got on the horse. The horse stood perfectly still and Alan kept him there for a few seconds while patting him and talking to him, letting the horse know that this was a safe place. He had already planned that when the horse bucked he would bring him back to the safe spot where they faced the sun, so the horse would not see this shadow with a monster on his back. Alan walked the horse a few steps then turned the horse's head to the left and the horse went into a frenzy of jumps and bucks. Alan's steadiness was effortless.

Billy heard one of the cowboys say, "He was the best and darn it if he still isn't the best at riding and taming wild horses." After a couple of wild runs around the corral Alan was able to bring the horse back to the safe spot and the horse calmed instantly. Alan took a couple more bucking rides around the arena always coming back to the safe spot and then turning the horse sideways while patting and talking to the horse. Suddenly the horse relaxed and let his head go down and exhaled noisily through his nose. The horse had overcome his fear and was trotting calmly. Alan took the horse around the corral another five times and always stopped on the safe spot. Each time the horse left the safe spot the Cowboys waited for some action and bucking, but the horse remained completely calm.

Alan said, "Billy come here, "Would you like to ride this horse?"

"Yes," said Billy. "Do you think I can ride him?"

"Yes I do." This vote of confidence from Alan, a man he already worshipped although he had known him for only a couple of days, was all he needed.

"Okay. I will ride the horse"

Alan sat Billy delicately on the horse and told Billy to pat the horse and talk to it. He let them walk around the corral. Alan said, "From now on this horse is your horse and you will have to find him a name." Thirty minutes ago none of these talented, tough cowboys could stay on the horse for more than thirty seconds. Now an eight-year-old kid was walking around safely on the same horse.

The cowboys were in awe and came to shake hands with Alan, expressing their admiration while Billy was beaming and telling everybody while walking on his horse, "This is my horse. Alan gave it to me."

Alan introduced Billy to these tough cowboys, who were his friends, and pointed out three of them to Billy, telling him that if Alan was not around, he should ask them for any help he might need.

Chapter 6: First Encounter with Clara

"Hey Billy, today we are going to another town. You'll be glad to know it's the town where I go most often and where I own a little barn and corral for my horses. You are going to meet the most extraordinary woman in the world. Her name is Clara and she lives with her daughter Judith, who is a little younger than you are. She is a widow. She lost her husband four years ago so don't ask anything about him."

They rode into town, Billy riding Flame, Alan's well-trained horse, and Alan riding Buddy, the new horse who needed more training. They went directly to a very large house which bore the sign: "Nightingale Boarding and Meals." They dismounted in front, tied their horses to the rail and were on the porch ready to enter when Billy saw a tall and beautiful woman step outside and hug Alan. "Glad to see you Alan! I saw you through the window, and I was eager to greet you and meet your little companion."

Alan answered, "That's Billy. We met on the trail. He is with me now learning to be a cowboy, I'll explain to you later."

"Well," said Clara, "I'm sure Judith will be very happy to meet him when she comes back from school at noon."

Clara walked through the house, leading them toward the kitchen where she put out some plates with bread, butter and milk and told them she was going to prepare them a really good meal for lunch and that they should sit down and make themselves comfortable.

Billy couldn't take his eyes off Clara. He thought she must be a princess because her eyes were deep blue, she had black hair and she was so tall that she seemed to move almost without walking. She was gliding through the room. Because she smiled a lot, Billy was not afraid of her, but he was completely mesmerized. Then Alan asked Billy to help him take the horses to the barn, brush them a little bit and give them water and food.

Judith came back from school before lunch, and after introductions they ate. Billy and Judith related to each other with a mixture of shyness and caution.

Chapter 7: Clara and her horses

Billy was very excited. They were all going to Clara's ranch, not very far from the town, at the base of the hills. Clara told them that they were leaving after lunch and would be at the ranch for dinner, spend the night and the next couple of days there and that she would show them her colts, mares, stallions and her prize horses. After a very pleasant ride with Clara and Alan, who were in a very good mood, they arrived a couple of hours before sunset. Clara gave them a short tour, showing them the few horses that were in the barn and next to the barn. She was very proud when she showed them what she called her two prize horses, Whispering Wind and Happy Jack. She explained to them that these two magnificent young horses, were the sons of the same stallion: Black Diamond, also named The Great One, who had been recognized by all competent horsemen in this part of the country as the most magnificent stallion of all, a very rare black stallion. Black Diamond was in a large pasture with prime grass a couple of miles from the barn along with some mares. Most of his sons and daughters were all black or dapple gray, with a few dark bays.

After the tour of the ranch, Clara and Alan went back inside to fix dinner. Judith stayed outside with Billy, showing him the horses she liked and things she enjoyed. Judith was a tomboy and challenged Billy at every turn, "You can't climb as high as I can in this tree." He would sometimes match her but not surpass her. Looking out through the kitchen's window, Alan could see that Billy was now a happy kid. The complete change of scenery, the days packed with action and Billy being around Alan's best friends made a huge difference

At dinner they all sat around the table and had a wonderful time. Everyone was happy and excited. There were two ranch hands on Clara's ranch, Chris and Pablo. Maria, Pablo's wife, had cooked a delicious rice pudding that the kids and the adults ate with great pleasure. Chris and Pablo had eaten earlier, but they came after dinner to share coffee and tell amazing tales about mountain lions and fights against Indians in the old days. After such a long day the two kids went to bed, after almost falling asleep at the table.

The next day they were all together, sitting and having lunch on the porch when they saw Chris coming on his horse at a dead run, stopping and dismounting at the same time. He went directly to Clara and exclaimed, "The Great One is gone! The fence is down and the stallion and all the mares are gone. I tracked around a little bit and I saw the tracks of six shod horses that were leading our herd of horses north, and I came back as soon as I could to warn you and organize a team to get the horses back."

Clara snapped out of her chair and told Chris and Pablo to return fully armed on fresh mounts. Then she asked Alan to saddle two horses, one for him and one for her. She went to get rifles and ammunition. She told Maria to bring water canteens, dry food, and blankets for each of the riders. She was perfectly in control.

She turned around and talked to Judith and Billy, "I am sorry about what is happening, kids, but while we go after these bandits who stole my horses you will have to stay with Maria who will take good care of you. I want you to be nice and do what Maria asks you to do."

"Let's get going and get after these thieves right away."

They started at a regular trot to warm up their horses and not exhaust them in the first few minutes. After a while they picked up a slow canter and discussed their strategy.

Clara said to Chris, "From what you told me, they are not very far away and they went north pushing the mares and the stallion as a group, because nobody but me can approach the stallion. My guess is they are going to try to box them in Deep Gulch Canyon, the only narrow canyon that is fit for that. I am going to take a gamble, cut across the hills and go directly to the canyon and hide at the very end. You try to catch up with them and when they get in the canyon you will be right behind them. If they take a different direction, send somebody to warn me."

They parted and this time both parties started at a strong canter. After a couple of hours of tracking, it was almost sundown, but the direction was definitively Deep Gulch

Canyon. The thieves appeared to be ahead by about four or five hours.

They decided to make camp early, take a quick break, let the horses drink and rest and then wake up at midnight and continue to gain on the horse thieves. They knew this part of the country extremely well, and the moonlight was sufficient for them to proceed at a walk and a trot.

In the meantime, Clara, riding one of her finest horses, headed to the canyon then skirted the entrance and went to the left side. With her horse she climbed to higher ground and walking parallel to the canyon she went on very slowly, studying every aspect of the canyon and trying to find the best spot to aim at the outlaws and another spot to completely hide her horse. She picketed her horse at the top of the canyon where there was some grass and a few trees. For herself she picked a spot behind a rock at the edge of the canyon. She had guessed right. She could see below her that the outlaws had built a crude fence, blocking the canyon and meant to trap the horses. It was a good choice because in addition to the narrowness of the canyon there was a little pond with a spring. She then went back to her viewpoint where she planned to spend the rest of the night with a blanket. She did not light a campfire in order not to reveal her position. She would be ready in the morning.

She had dozed for a couple of hours when she heard her herd and the bandits coming into the canyon.

Alan, Chris and Pablo had started to ride at midnight. Now it was a full moon, and they could see that the tracks of the stolen horses were fresh. Climbing on the right to the top of the canyon just as dawn broke, they could make out the stolen horses trapped in Deep Gulch Canyon. It was a well-made trap; bushes and rocks had been erected as a barrier to prevent the horses from going all the way to the other end of the canyon. They could not see Clara, so they guessed that she was on the other side of the canyon. There was only one thing really wrong: there were not six riders but about twelve. Another troop of outlaws had joined the others and were staying at the entrance of the canyon, invisible to Clara.

Alan told Pablo and Chris, "Clara will be discovered by so many men, and of course, knowing her she will shoot at the thieves anyway without knowing they are so many. One group of outlaws can go around and behind her while the others can keep us busy by shooting at us. She will be shot to pieces

by the outlaws sneaking up behind her so now
we really have to think hard."

Chapter 8: Rescuing Clara's horses

The only way to rescue her was to act quickly and boldly and go after the outlaws together. The only way to be fast in this situation was for him to use his old circus skills.

He, Chris, and Pablo were on the other side of the canyon. They could see Clara across the canyon, and they believed she could see them because of the faint light from dawn. As fast as he could, Alan tied his rope and Chris' and Pablo's ropes together and because they were going after a herd, Pablo had brought extra ropes.

Alan gestured to Clara to be silent and then threw his rope across the canyon; Clara caught the rope and understood that she had to tie her side of the rope to a boulder. With

Pablo's help, Alan fastened the other end tightly around a tree. He had only minutes before the sun rose. Too much light would make him visible and would make it impossible to rescue Clara.

Alan climbed onto the rope wearing his soft moccasins and walked down to where Clara was standing. He changed direction on the rope, swooped Clara up in his arms, sat her on his shoulders and began to walk back on the rope towards their friends, as always Clara was game but walking the rope with a woman on his shoulders was very difficult. His arms were extended, his knees were slightly bent. More than once he had to recover his balance. The best way to do that was to stay with one leg on the rope and keep the other leg off the rope and raise the leg and lower it as a very efficient counter-weight. He learned to use this recovery move years ago at the Circus. It was the most difficult exercise of tight-rope walking he had ever done and in addition the rope was not tight enough. In fact the rope was rather slack and twice he almost lost his balance. When he got to the middle of the rope it was already daylight and the outlaws were beginning to cook their breakfast without noticing that two flying human beings were right above their heads.

Finally Alan and Clara jumped safely onto terra firma.

The next question was "How can we rescue the horses?"

Clara said to Alan, Pablo, and Chris, "I have to make an example that will scare these horse thieves, an example that will become a legend and be repeated throughout the west. It is the only way for me as a woman to be safe. If word of mouth spreads the news that I am very bad medicine for thieves, I will be safe for many years. It's worth taking a few risks."

As they watched the horse thieves, they recognized the leader of the two groups. The first group, the one that had captured the horses, was led by a slim man with blond hair and a large scar across his cheek that gave him a frightening appearance. He was also giving orders to the second group as they reunited. Now that the thieves were sharing breakfast, both groups were together, a good dozen of them in the open.

Clara told Alan, Pablo and Chris that she would go alone and challenge the leader by herself, but she planned to stand near a large boulder were she could take refuge after the shooting started. Alan, Pablo and Chris would take positions on the ridge of the canyon and would be ready to shoot at the thieves. Clara said, "I will wait until you get to your positions. Do not shoot until I start shooting. I will take care of the leader while you keep the rest busy."

When not in town, Clara always wore a gun, its holster tied around her thigh. She checked her colt to make sure it was loaded and that it was free in the holster. For any other woman, going into the outlaw's den and facing them alone would have been the act of a crazy woman. It was almost a surrealistic scene, but the men around her knew that she was in control and that her plan was, as always, well thought out.

Clara walked silently toward the outlaws. They did not notice her at first. Loudly she said, "Hello my dear friends. You know that it is very bad to steal horses. These horses are mine and I am taking them back. Drop your guns now." In the meantime she kept her sights on the leader. The leader turned towards her and was going to speak while dropping his hand to his gun when Alan's booming voice then Pablo's and Chris' voices were heard from places invisible to the outlaws, sternly ordering the outlaws to, "Drop your guns and raise your hands."

Two outlaws raised their gun and bullets from Alan and Pablo drilled holes through each of their heads.

The other outlaws froze but did not drop their guns. Clara and Alan knew that it would take more aggressive action to make them drop their guns.

Clara addressed the leader, "You the coward, the horse thief, I challenge you to draw and shoot me before I put a hole in your ugly mug. You have your chance. I am armed. I have not drawn yet and my friends will not shoot you. If you don't take your chance you are the worst coward in the entire world, a man who does not have the guts to draw against a woman." The leader went for his gun at once and as his gun cleared his holster, his motion stopped and two neat holes appeared on his shirt right were his heart was. He was dead before he reached the ground.

Her fast draw was smooth and perfect. At the same time she shot the leader, other outlaws raised their guns, but Allen, Chris, and Pablo shot them dead. The lightning speed of Clara's draw had a magical effect, and the outlaws who had not drawn their guns dropped their weapons and raised their hands very high. Clara told them, "You have seen that I am the fastest gun in the region. I should hang you and you know it but I will let you go and from now on, not only you will not steal my horses, but you will protect the horses you see with my brand the double C. Get your horses and go now! I had the time to have a good look at you and if you come close to my ranch or my town I will shoot you without any warning and my friends will do the same." While Clara was talking, Allen had picked up all of the rifles and revolvers as well as cartridge belts while Chris and Pablo remained hidden behind boulders. The outlaws mounted their horses, took their dead companions with them and left. Clara, Alan, Chris, and Pablo pushed the small herd out of the canyon and drove the stallion and his mares gently back to the ranch where they arrived the next day.

Chapter 9: The Shooting contest

When they returned to Clara's ranch, they put the horses back into a secure pasture and joined the kids who were delighted to see them. Clara reminded everybody that this coming Sunday after church there was the annual shooting contest as well as a small rodeo and dancing at the end of the day. All this excitement would be accompanied by barbecues and pies and games for the kids. Everybody in town except for a few grouches would participate in at least one of the activities.

It was obvious that Clara was very excited about the important annual social event. Part of the excitement was that people came from far away to enjoy the entertainment.

Billy asked Alan what he would be doing and Alan answered, "Enjoying myself."

"But doing what?" asked Billy

"Dancing and eating pies"

Billy was surprised. "You are not going to enter the shooting contest or the rodeo?"

"No."

'Why?"

"You will see that my best friend is going to enter the shooting contest, and I don't want to compete against my best friend. For the rodeo, I have competed so many times that it's not exciting anymore."

The good news for you is that you and Judith will be with me all day long and we'll have a lot of fun."

"Are we going to see the shooting contest and the rodeo?" asked Billy

"Yes, of course."

"OK," said Billy, and he ran out with Judith both of them yelling that they were going to the shooting contest tomorrow.

The next day, the shooting contest started at noon and to Billy's surprise, Clara was a contestant. She was given the honor of being the first to shoot. With her rifle she put three bullets dead center in a small circle 100 feet away. It was the first challenge designed to eliminate half of the contestants, who were quite numerous. The contest took almost two hours.

While the other contestants continued the elimination round, she took her guests to a large table under a tree where ladies were serving the pies that won the contest in the morning. It was indeed a very good day, Billy reflected as he ate three portions of three different pies, outdoing Judith in the process. Judith called him a pig.

They walked back to the shooting contest for the next part of the competition. The shooting was becoming more interesting now. The targets were three different circles the size of a silver dollar. Clara again shot a perfect score and was up for the next round. Billy was hypnotized by the noise, the smells, and the accuracy of many of the shooters. In the meantime Clara and Alan were greeting old friends they had not seen since the year before.

Only ten contestants had succeeded in qualifying for the next round. The next contest was to shoot three copper coins set on a rail 100 yards away. Clara and one other contestant sent the three copper coins flying in the air. Now it was a one on one, a crowd favorite.

Clara was the darling of the town against a stranger who happened to pass through town. The stranger was elegant and dressed mostly in black.

He saluted Clara and said, "Coming to this neck of the woods I would never have thought that I would be challenged rifle in hand by such a lovely lady. Allow me to offer you the victory as a token of my admiration."
Clara answered, "The victory is not yours yet, you have not won and your gift is as empty as your words. Try for once to win fair and square against a woman." Clara's answer drew cheers and applause from the crowd.

The next round was a brilliant test. One hundred yards away and hanging from one of the highest branches of an oak tree were two little boxes containing one playing card. Each of these little boxes could be opened by shooting the twig that held them closed which would allow the card inside the box to fall gracefully to the ground. The challenge was then to put as many bullets as possible through the falling card. The contestant who opened the box and put the most holes in the card before it touched the ground would win. The public liked to watch this round because they could count the shots and see the card jump when hit by a bullet.

The draw had Clara shooting first. Clara seemed to make the card dance with her shots and the entire crowd counted aloud four shots, all of which hit the card.

It was the stranger's turn. He fired an incredible number of shots before the card touched the ground, four of which drilled holes in his card.

It was an even contest. In the past, the box and card trial had never failed to decide the winner. The organizer of the contest stepped in and challenged the contestants to split a card showing only its edge from 100 yards. The card would be set in a twig showing only its profile which at 100 feet looked as thin as a hair. Each contestant would only be allowed one bullet. The stranger snickered and Alan asked him if he wanted to withdraw. The stranger answered, "Please place the cards." The Stranger aimed carefully, shot and missed.

Then Clara shot and split her card in two pieces that fell to the ground. Clara was declared the winner and the entire crowd surrounded their lady who had vanquished the stranger. The ladies hugged her, the men shook her hand.

The stranger in anger shouted to the crowd, "The lady was lucky! Nobody can make that shot!" His words were a grave insult to their heroine.

Alan stepped in, put his cold, piercing eyes on the stranger and said, "In addition to being a skunk who insults women I would like to know if you are also a coward. Walk over there and we will draw against each other." Looking into Alan's eyes, the stranger saw that he was going to die.

Alan had observed during the shooting contest that while everybody was carrying only a rifle, his challenger was wearing in addition a gun belt with a beautiful six shooter at his side, the holster tied down to his left thigh with the butt of the gun to the right. The gun belt was tied low at an angle that showed a good knowledge of guns and gunfights. Alan's power of observation and his ability to read animal and human behavior and character was the reason that Alan was still alive after having confronted so many dangers in an adventure-filled life. Alan's gun was tied down too, very low on his right leg and his right hand would fall naturally toward the butt of his gun.

The stranger made the choice to stay alive and said, "I apologize to the lady." He turned around, mounted his horse, and left.

Then they all went to the rodeo. Judith and Billy had a great time, when back at the ranch, Billy could not restrain himself from saying to Clara that he admired her almost as much as he admired Alan: "You are the best shooter in the world."

Clara said, "Billy you are very kind, but Alan was my teacher and he is a great shooter."

Billy interjected, "Alan, when we were camping you were going to tell me how you became good at shooting when you were working in the shooting gallery." Clara and Judith wanted to listen to the story too.

Chapter 10: Alan's Shooting Skills

Alan said, "OK Billy, you deserve to hear the rest of the story at the shooting gallery ."

This is the story Alan told.

"On a Friday afternoon, a gentleman about forty years old came in. I noticed he was limping. He told the owner that he would be shooting for the prize. In fact we had a $1.00 prize for any customer using a hand gun who could put five bullets into a target the size of a silver dollar a hundred feet from the shooter.

The first time the gentleman -whose first name was James- shot at the target, he got the prize. He shot again and got the prize again. He then shot again and again got the prize, three times in a row. The owner was beginning to get upset.

After collecting his money, James left. He came back the following Friday afternoon and again he won the prize, this time four times in a row. He was very nice to me and let me load his gun. The owner told him that the next time he came he could not compete for the prize money. This gentleman then told the owner that he would come next Friday and that not only would he show him a new handgun but that he would explain a way to make a lot of money.

The next Friday James came with what he called a Colt revolver. He showed the gun to Mr. Smith who had heard about this gun but had never seen one. Now James, whom I began to consider my friend because he was very nice to me, shot six bullets in less than six seconds into the small target using the Colt revolver. I was amazed and so was the owner. You could shoot six bullets in less than six seconds without any reloading.

He then told the owner that this Colt revolver was the future and that he should sell it to his customers. James told the owner that he would help him the following Friday by demonstrating the quality of this revolver while winning prize money. James then said to Mr. Smith: 'Buy some Colt revolvers, put some posters around town, hand out some leaflets, talk to everybody around and you will have a crowd next Friday. I know it will work because when I was working in a small circus I learned how to get people excited about coming to our circus. Write in your leaflets that you have the most modern, accurate handguns of all and that these guns can shoot six times in less than six seconds and hit a silver dollar six times in a row at a distance of 100 feet.'

The next Friday, fifty people were waiting to be shown the Colt revolver. James was magnificent. Of course he never missed a shot. Now everybody wanted to try and the owner sold all the Colt revolvers he had. But because he was a cautious man, he had bought only five Colt revolvers. He told us later that if he had had twenty revolvers, he would have sold twenty.

Every Friday afternoon, Mr. Smith the owner and James the skilled shooter paired up and sold revolvers.

It could seem that there was not much for me to gain, but in fact I benefited enormously from these two men. They were willing to share their knowledge with me, and I was a curious young man and an avid learner. James explained to me that even if you are the best in the world at something but nobody knows it, you will become a useless, bitter recluse or a source of irritation for your family and friends. He told me: 'The golden rule is made of three steps: Not only be extremely good at what you do, but also be enthusiastic and passionate about what you do which will give you the strength to put very long hours into your endeavors, next you must make the world aware of your talents and your ethics . That is all there is to being successful in life. It is a very simple proposition, but few people are able to focus with indomitable determination and enthusiasm to implement these three steps.'

He then told me that he had been a captain in the Union Army during the Civil War and was given a Colt revolver as his side arm. He had been wounded at the end of the war and he was recovering, but now that the war was over he would probably be discharged soon. He also told me that before the war he worked in a circus riding horses and shooting at targets and that is where he learned to become a good shooter. James explained to me that one of the stars of the circus who was a remarkable shooter hired him to quickly load the guns he was using while shooting at different targets held by a beautiful lady. Of course at this time the Colt revolver was not available.

The people working in the circus have a tradition because there is no circus school. These circus artists strive to pass along their art and talent to young people and I was one of the lucky one who benefited from this tradition.

'Billy, because I was lucky and blessed to learn a difficult skill, I will pass along to you what my mentor James taught me because it is the fair thing to do. In addition I must tell you that I like you because of your enthusiasm.' James told me that he had another three months of recovery and that he would come and train me not only on Friday but also on Wednesday in the afternoon to help the owner make more money. In exchange, James told me that he would ask the owner to give me bullets, powder, and shells so that I could practice more often.

One day he told me he would take me the following Sunday afternoon to the circus where he had been an apprentice and where some of his friends worked. The next Sunday we went to the circus and I was mesmerized by many of the artists, especially the tight-rope walker and the trick horses.

After the show, James introduced me to his friends as well as the manager of the circus and while he was talking of the good old times, the sons, daughters, and apprentices of his friends gave me a tour of the circus that included many horses and some strange animals. They also offered me to work with them and learn many circus tricks. An offer I gladly accepted because I saw a member of the Circus who was training shoot at a target while riding a horse at the canter, something that exited me a lot.

At seventeen I was a man already blessed by the kindness of three talented persons. It was already a great gift in life.

James had to leave. After he left and for a short period, I demonstrated the Colt revolver to future customers. When they saw that Alan a seventeen-year-old boy could put six bullets in a target the size of a silver dollar, customers bought a lot of Colt revolvers and the owner Mr. Smith was happy. Then I joined the circus and worked very hard at learning these difficult skills"

Chapter 11: Meeting a Friendly Indian Tribe

The next day Alan told Billy that they were going to ride for a few days and asked him to get his horse ready.

"We are going to meet some Indians from one of the Plains tribes. I know them and they are friendly, but there is another tribe that is new to the region and I would like to meet them. It is always good to try to get to know them before you have an unexpected encounter with them in the wild. There is a small village a few miles north, and we are going there to see if they welcome us. We will try to stay only a short time and impress them with some tricks I have in my bags. These are friendly Indians, so don't be afraid. If we make a good and strong impression on them, our reputation of strong and fair men will spread to other Indian tribes."

Alan and Billy entered a village with about twenty teepees. They were greeted by curious dogs and kids until finally half a dozen warriors came to meet them. Alan asked one of the older warriors in a mixture of English, Indian language, and Spanish if he could talk with the Chief, making sure they knew he had come with peaceful intentions. After so many years roaming the Indian territories, he could understand many Indian languages and was almost able to speak them fluently.

The Chief, a tall, obviously strong man probably in his fifties, came and began to talk, and some of the translation was done in the same mixture of different languages, with some added hand signs from one of the warriors.

Alan told the Chief that he had heard about his bravery and that he was going to live in the area, and that he was, himself a great warrior and a great medicine man. Alan told the Chief that he wanted to be their friend and that he could provide them with knives, hatchets, and tools in exchange for some animal pelts. The Chief expressed no apparent interest.

Alan asked the Chief if he could compete against three of his best archers because he, Alan, was the best archer on the plains. Alan added that a good competition is always a way to make a day pleasant, and if he lost he would give one knife to each warrior that competed and a long double-edge knife to the Chief. If he won he would like to receive the skin of a deer.

The warriors were getting excited and talking back and forth. The Chief agreed to Alan's challenge and four targets made of bark painted red, each the size of a large bird, were set up on tree trunks a hundred feet away. After some talking, he understood that they were to use three arrows each. They were to shoot one after the other, and he was to shoot last. All the warriors were ready. The whole camp was there to watch.

He told Billy, "You are going to act as my helper and you will pass me different items when I call their names. When the Indians see you helping me, they will think you're an apprentice medicine man."

Alan went to his saddlebag and pulled out the different parts needed to assemble his crossbow. He did that to impress the Indians and succeeded. He gave some parts to Billy who handed them to him when asked.

He first removed the bow and the arrows, and then, when the tribe was watching him he took the cross and fitted the bow on its frame and raised his hand to show it to the tribe. There was much curiosity and many comments. The warriors gathered around him and touched the crossbow. He explained again that he was a great warrior and medicine man, that it was his sacred weapon.

Because he knew that the target and the distance had been chosen to accommodate the Indian warriors, he was not surprised that each of them scored an almost perfect score. None had missed the target but their arrows were not in the center of the target.

He then went to face the target one hundred yards away, and in less than one minute put three arrows dead center in the target. Once on the target, his arrows touched each other and the accuracy at which he was able to let the arrows fly drew whispers of admiration. He then told the Chief that if the Chief agreed and because it was an even contest, he would be very pleased to give the knives to the warriors and to the Chief and to receive in exchange a deer skin as gestures of friendship. The Chief was pleased, and invited him and Billy to eat with him.

The Chief was intrigued by the crossbow and as he held it and looked it over Alan told him that only he could make it work because he was from a faraway country where his ancestors used this crossbow.

As they were walking away from the target area toward the center of the village, when they were about three hundred feet from the targets, he turned around and told the Chief his power was very strong, that he could kill at a greater distance than anybody else. He put an arrow in his crossbow, and sent the arrow dead center into one of the targets. This time the Chief and the other warriors were even more impressed. Then they sat around talking and sharing stories and food and drink was offered to them. The ambiance was friendly.

Billy shadowed Alan's every move. Alan insisted that all the tribes and all the warriors the Chief knew must be made aware that him the man with the magic bow, and his young son Billy were powerful men but also friendly men and must be respected as such.

Billy was an attraction by himself because of his pale blond hairs and was shy and nervous when members of the tribe wanted to touch him. Alan took him aside and told him to go and play with the son of the chief who was his age. To make Billy comfortable, Alan organized a jumping contest for some of the kids. All of the children were soon running, jumping, having a good time.

Chapter 12: The Fight with Young Beaver

Alan was enjoying the meal and the beginning of a friendship with the Chief when a young warrior with a sour face who was jealous of Alan's success addressed him harshly. "You are too good with your special weapon that kills from far away. It allows you to avoid real fighting You are too much of a coward to fight very close with a knife like a real man"

The Chef barked, "You young scoundrel, this man is a guest and you are very rude, go away before I expel you from the tribe."

The young warrior turned around but muttered loud enough to be heard by the spectators, "This man is a coward." The crowd knew that although the young warrior whose name was Young Beaver was very rude, the white man who was their guest had to answer. Alan wanted to help the chief in this difficult situation. He faced the crowd and addressed them telling the crowd that it was a nice afternoon and we are all having a good time and your chief who is a wise man is protecting me the guest of the tribe, he is a man of honor."

"But I cannot let a young skunk insult me and say that I am a coward, I will fight him in a close fight one on one, but because it is a friendly afternoon and I do not want any blood spilled I am challenging this young warrior to a fight in Indian wrestling" and he shouted the last two words, "Indian wrestling."

He heard the crowd loudly approve what he said and then the Chief said, "The white man is a brave man and he will fight the young skunk. He is also a wise man because he does not want blood to be spilled on the ground on the day of a friendly gathering.

Alan could see that Billy was worried and was close to tears. He took Billy to the Chief who was with his young son and asked the chief to promise to take Billy to the nearest town, the one the Indian called "the little busy place" if something bad happened to him. The Chief promised, and Billy felt better.

Alan took Billy aside and told him, "Billy you should not worry, when I was in France a year before I left I was in Paris and every day I went to the most famous school of French Boxing lead by the great Master Charles Lecour. It is a very effective boxing technique."

Alan concealed a concern: he was over fifty years old and the young warrior was in his early twenties and almost a giant.

The chief drew a large circle in the sand and the contestants got ready. The crowd was excited.

The Chief said that the fight will end either at first blood or when one contestant did not get up or when he the Chief stopped the fight.

Alan took his shirt off, put his gun belt over Billy's shoulder, and entered the circle at the same time the Indian warrior did. Young Beaver was the name the crowd has given to the young warrior.

The Chief gave the signal and Alan and Young Beaver began to circle each other.

Alan moved right slightly to bait his opponent and the young warrior lunged at Alan trying to take him in a deadly embrace.

Alan sidestepped left while slapping hard and fast with an open hand on his opponent's right shoulder to push him aside and at the same time he punched him hard with a right hook to the midsection. Young Beaver did not even notice the blow.

Alan realized that Young Beaver wanted to kill him and that is why he tried the deadly embrace in order to break his back. He also realized that this man was one in a million and that this man had rare stamina and resilience. It was going to be a difficult fight. Alan knew he was fighting for his life.

It was a bare-hand fight, but his powerful opponent was a predator, a beast who had only one way of dealing with his opponents: killing them. In fact half of the human beings on earth were predators intent on destroying or harming the other half who were born prey. These human predators use any means to win, were contemptuous of the law, and willing to use any means to win. Only the rise of democracy when well applied had given weapons for the ones who were born prey to unite and organize a world where they could live, create, and prosper. That world would be a world were human predators would be kept in check by the majority of citizens and their laws, their judges, sheriffs, and lawyers. Today he was in a lawless land in a fight to the finish with the ultimate predator---a powerful killer.

He realized that his only chance was to hit him with his feet, his knees, and his elbow and above all to stay away from his embrace while constantly baiting him in order to keep the advantage of guiding the fight into his own kind of fight.

Alan feinted a right uppercut to the midsection and the young warrior dropped his right arm to protect his stomach and leaned forward a little bit, Alan unleashed a hard kick with his left foot to the warrior's head, a picture perfect kick of the school of French boxing called La Savate which uses legs and arms, with a preference for kicking with the legs.

The young warrior went flying while the crowd could hear the thud of the impact of Alan's feet on the warrior head. On any other man that would have been a knockout blow. The young warrior fell but immediately bounced back. He did not rise slowly but jumped back on his feet and went on the attack, surprising Alan.

This time the young warrior tried to grab Alan's neck, and only a quick side step allowed Alan to avoid his deadly grip. But the nails of his opponent scratched his neck and he began bleeding.

The Chief stood up and interposed himself between the two opponents declaring that the "friendly contest" was over because blood has been spilled.

Alan knew he could not accept. He turned to the crowd and asked them, "Want the fight to continue?" and the crowd roared, "Yes!"

He then said to the Chief, "You were right to stop the fight because blood was spilled but it is only a scratch, and I beg you to let us continue the fight until one stays on the ground."

The Chief, a very experienced man who by now understood that the young warrior was bent on killing Alan, had no choice but to allow the fight to continue. He told Alan, "You are a very brave man but also a fool."

Alan looked at Billy and saw in fear and despair in the boy's eyes. This insight into the soul of Billy gave Alan the utter determination to win no matter what.

He was no longer a man in a fight for his life; he was a man fighting for the soul and the future of an eight-year-old boy who had just lost his parents. A feeling of power came over him. Fighting for a cause is so much more powerful than fighting for one's life.

Alan entered the circle and the crowd became silent. From Alan an aura of utter determination could be felt by every spectator. The Chief gave the signal. Alan saw that his opponent was more cautious, which gave Alan more time to bait and feint. It also made his opponent more unpredictable.

Determined to keep the initiative, Alan moved forward, side-stepped, and delivered a powerful kick to Young Beaver's knee. The young buck fell, but this time Alan stayed close to him, and when the young warrior rose, Alan unleashed another sidekick to his opponent's leg sending him to the ground again.

This young warrior would not quit. From a crouch, with one of his legs almost destroyed, Young beaver lunged at Alan like a wounded lion.

Alan jumped back but the young buck grabbed Alan's left arm and pulled Alan towards him.

Instead of trying to free his arm Alan hit the Warrior's throat with his right elbow which made the warrior release Alan's arm.

Although the young buck had one injured knee Alan knew that the young man could still kill him if his neck or spine was caught in this warrior's embrace.

Young Beaver lunged again, and Alan hit him with a side kick and the warrior fell on his face. Alan sat on his back and put his arm around his neck to strangle him. Alan began to squeeze with all the strength he had. The warrior went thrashing and jumping and rolling but Alan kept his deadly grip on the warrior's throat. Young Beaver stood up using his good leg. Alan had dug his heels into the warrior's flank and then began the wildest ride of his life. He was riding a superhuman monster. Immune to the pain and wounds in his knee, the warrior was crashing Alan against boulders and trees. It was the most dangerous rodeo Alan had ever experienced. The young warrior had such strong throat muscles that Alan with all his strength was barely able to compress Young Beaver's throat, the young warrior fought for what felt like an eternity with the crowd screaming and yelling. After what seemed to Alan a very long time, the warrior began to slow down but in a fearsome burst of energy he sent Alan flying against a boulder.

Alan was weakening and knew that it was now or never. He had to bait the warrior into a final trap. A complicated move he had invented, which relied on perfect timing. He feinted a right hook to the warrior's face, and as the Indian warrior raised his hands Alan dropped and grabbed the warrior's right ankle, then stood up and started to spin his body. He spun faster and faster which made the body of Little Beaver go horizontal. Alan slammed the warrior against a boulder face first and then, changing direction spun a couple of times to gain speed and then slammed the warrior against the same boulder but with the back of the head first. Incredibly, the warrior was still moving. Alan gathered more speed in his rotations and again slammed the body of the warrior full force against the boulder. This time the body of the warrior went limp and Alan let go, knowing that he had won. Alan walked closer to the unconscious warrior and was relieved to hear the warrior breathing. Alan turned toward the chief and told him, "Your young warrior will live although he wanted to kill me. I could have killed him, but I let him live and he will become a wiser man in the future and you and I will remain friends". While talking to the chief, Alan observed Billy who was not crying. He was standing tall and smiling. Alan felt proud of Billy. Alan now knew that Billy was becoming a strong young man and an asset to the community.

Alan said to Billy, "Let's go. I need some rest and care. Let's go back to Clara and Judith. I am too old for this kind of Fandango. I need the care and love of my friend and you will be able to play with Judith."

Billy went to the horses, which had remained saddled. He put Alan's saddlebags on them and brought the three horses to Alan. They saluted the chief who saluted them and they left the village.

While riding back to Clara's ranch, Alan reflected on the immense wave of power and happiness that surged in him when he realized that now he was the protector of a defenseless young boy. Until then he had not understood the meaning of the word "cause" but now he had a cause and it was the most powerful feeling he ever had experienced. As Billy's protector he knew now that he could overcome any challenge the world could throw at him.

The End
Eric Lafayette

More Information for my readers:

As one of my readers you are welcome to share your thoughts on my website: www.ericlafayette.com

What would a book written by Eric Lafayette be without a good measure of his philosophy as well as some inspiration from other masters of incisive, short bits of wisdom?

Both Clara and Alan live by the following quotes:

Winston Churchill

"Never give in, never give in, never; never; never; never - in nothing, great or small, large or petty - never give in except to convictions of honor and good sense"

Here is my favorite as it is so well coined:
Winston Churchill

"Success is the ability to go from failure to failure without losing your enthusiasm"

Albert Einstein

"Insanity is doing the same thing over and over again and expecting different results"

Finding out why we are born and thus what meaning we can give to our life will make you and your friends extremely happy.
Mark Twain

"The two most important days of our life are the day you are born and the day you find out why."

Thomas Edison

"I have not failed. I've just found 10,000 ways that won't work"

We are proud to offer you a quick description of Eric Lafayette poems, books and essays:

Book, Philosophical poem by Eric Lafayette

The next book to be published in 2014 is:
The Greatest Military Commanders and Diplomats in History (provisional title)
An extremely brilliant book on the amazing and very different Strategies and tactics that Alexander the Great, Hannibal, Julius Caesar, Genghis Khan, Napoleon, " Overwhelming force" and Sun Tzu used to be almost invincible.
These talented military commanders as well as a few gifted diplomats redefined and redesigned part of our planet in the past centuries.
Excerpt:
ALEXANDER THE GREAT (356-323 BC)

Alexander's signature strategy was charge and charge again. Charging like a possessed man at the head of his elite troops was Alexander the Great's signature strategy. Alexander's strategy was a direct result of his culture as well as his personal bravery. He came from a cast of warriors whose culture focused on heroism and absolute bravery. It is very important to underline that

Alexander the Great had formalized into an ubber elite group his friends-soldiers that were officially named " Companions". His group of companions all cavalry were not only ready to die for him. but they had to show by relentless attacks and acts of bravery that they were as brave as Alexander and the bar was very, very high because Alexander was the bravest. Using the hyper macho culture of his time Alexander had fashioned the most aggressive talented, small elite attack troop into a formidable tactical weapon.

Next writing, a Poem already available :

Excerpt:

-You will be a woman-

A one page philosophical poem whose goal is to emulate for women the Rudyard Kipling Poem: " If ... You will be a man my son" with bits of wisdom and strong incitation for women to fight for their rights and have a great life.

Here are some free verses from the Poem:

"-When you say that a woman's life is full of challenges and you meet them all with joy and passion

-When you say I am not a man's equal but his superior in many fields

-When you know that you must fight for Democracy and put your belief in Democracy above all other beliefs

-When you spot people who are evil and stupid, fight them but accept innocent fools and love the intelligent

-When you do not yield to today's trends, to pressures from your environment or to the pressures of your peers

-When you harvest knowledge enthusiastically knowing that ignorance is the mother of all misfortunes"

Where can I find Eric Lafayette's books?

All books, Poems and essays are available at Amazon.com at the Eric Lafayette Internet store. "Eric Lafayette"(between quotation marks) or without the quotation marks for a general display
Or go to www.ericlafayette.com and order your books

If you liked this book and you believe this book will bring great satisfaction to other people you can write a good review on the book's page on Amazon.com

www.ingramcontent.com/pod-product-compliance
Lightning Source LLC
Chambersburg PA
CBHW070533130626
46555CB00003B/1399